The Twelve Days of
Christmas

Illustrated by Luis Filella

MILES
KELLY

On the first day of Christmas my true love gave to me,

a partridge in a pear tree.

On the second day of Christmas my true love gave to me,

two turtle doves

and a partridge in a pear tree.

On the third day of Christmas
my true love gave to me,

three French hens,

two turtle doves
and a partridge in
a pear tree.

On the fourth day of Christmas
my true love gave to me,

four calling birds,

three French hens,
two turtle doves
and a partridge in
a pear tree.

On the **fifth** day of Christmas
my true love gave to me,

five gold rings,

four calling birds, three French hens,
two turtle doves and
a partridge in a pear tree.

On the **sixth** day of Christmas
my true love gave to me,

six geese a-laying,

five gold rings, four calling birds,
three French hens, two turtle doves
and a partridge in a pear tree.

Six geese a-laying, five gold rings,
four calling birds, three French hens,
two turtle doves and
a partridge in a pear tree.

On the eighth day of Christmas
my true love gave to me,
eight maids a-milking,

Seven swans a-swimming,
Six geese a-laying,
five gold rings, four calling birds,
three French hens, two turtle doves
and a partridge in a pear tree.

On the ninth day of Christmas
my true love gave to me,

nine ladies dancing,
eight maids a-milking,
seven swans a-swimming,

On the tenth day of Christmas
my true love gave to me,

ten lords
a-leaping,

nine ladies dancing,
eight maids a-milking,

Seven swans a-swimming,
six geese a-laying,
five gold rings, four calling birds,
three French hens, two turtle doves
and a partridge in a pear tree.

On the eleventh day of Christmas
my true love gave to me,

eleven pipers piping,

ten lords a-leaping,
nine ladies dancing,

eight maids a-milking, seven swans a-swimming,
six geese a-laying, five gold rings,
four calling birds, three French hens,
two turtle doves and a partridge in a pear tree.

Six geese a-laying, five gold rings, four calling birds,
three French hens, two turtle doves
and a partridge in a pear tree.